JENNIFER NORTHWAY has written and illustrated a number of acclaimed picture books. Her book *Get Lost, Laura!* was shortlisted for the Smarties Award. In addition to her own stories, Jennifer has illustrated books for many well-known authors, including Jill Paton Walsh, Floella Benjamin and Mary Hoffman. Her book with Mary Hoffman, *Nancy No-Size*, was also shortlisted for the Smarties Award. Her work has been televised in England and all over Europe on children's programmes, and in New Zealand and Australia. She wrote and illustrated *See You Later, Mum*, also published by Frances Lincoln.

For Amy and Michael William – J.N.

Text and illustrations copyright © Jennifer Northway 1997
The right of Jennifer Northway to be identified as the author of this work has been asserted by
her in accordance with the Copyright, Designs and Patents Act, 1988 (United Kingdom).

This edition published in Great Britain in 2008 by
Frances Lincoln Children's Books, 4 Torriano Mews,
Torriano Avenue, London NW5 2RZ
www.franceslincoln.com

British Library Cataloguing in Publication Data available on request

ISBN 978-1-84507-896-6

Printed in Singapore

1 3 5 7 9 8 6 4 2

Lucy's Quarrel

Jennifer Northway

F

FRANCES LINCOLN
CHILDREN'S BOOKS

"My mum says I can choose all the games at my party," said Lucy to her cousin Alice, "and everyone has to do what I tell them, because it's my party!"

Alice was tired of hearing Lucy going on and on about her party. "That's just bossy!" she grumbled. "You're always bossy!"

"Me?" exclaimed Lucy. "We never do anything I want. We always play what you want... you're the bossy one – everyone says so!"

Alice stuck her tongue out at Lucy, so Lucy stuck her tongue out at Alice. "You're not my best friend any more," shouted Lucy. "And I don't want you to come to my party, so there!"

Alice was very upset. She ran downstairs to her mum…
…and she wouldn't say goodbye to Lucy when they went home.
She didn't try to make up. Nor did Lucy.

"You shouldn't quarrel like that and not make up," said Granny the next day. She was making Lucy's birthday cake. "Why don't you both say you're sorry? After all, she is your best friend, and your party is only a few days away."

"She isn't my friend any more!" said Lucy crossly,
"She started it, and she didn't say she was sorry!
And I don't want a chocolate cake for my birthday,
because that's Alice's favourite!"

"But it's your favourite too," said Granny.
"I don't care," said Lucy. "I want a lemon one now."

When Lucy saw Alice at playschool, Alice looked as if she wanted to be friends. But Lucy was still cross. She played in the kitchen with Peter.

Alice started playing with Emma and wouldn't look at Lucy.
Lucy knew Alice didn't like Emma very much because she was
a cry-baby.

After a while Lucy missed playing with Alice and began to feel
a bit like crying herself... but she wasn't going to say sorry!

The next day was Thursday. Alice and Lucy always did gym together on Thursdays. But this time Alice didn't come. Lucy jumped about to the music and did rolypolies, but it wasn't nearly so much fun without Alice.

As she didn't have a partner, she had to do headstands against a wall while the others did them in pairs.

After gym, Lucy and Mum bought lots of nice things to eat at the party.

"Alice likes tomato and bacon crisps best," said Lucy.

"Let's get them for her then," said Mum. "Pop them in the trolley."

"But she's not coming!" said Lucy, crossly.

"Well, you might change your mind by the time the party comes," said Mum.

"I won't!" snapped Lucy and dumped the crisps back on the shelf.

Lucy and Dad blew up lots of balloons.

"I want to play musical bumps, and statues," said Lucy.
"And that dressing-up race with all those clothes."

"Alice loves that game – she always wins," laughed Dad.
"Have you two made up yet?"

"No! And I'm not going to!" said Lucy. "She said I was bossy!"

"Well, you are sometimes," said Dad. "You're both bossy –
it's a shame to spoil your party over a silly quarrel."

Lucy began to feel sad. "I don't think my birthday's going to be much fun," she sighed to Mum. "I wish I hadn't quarrelled with Alice. I wish we were still friends."

"Why don't you make it up?" said Mum. "It's not so hard to say sorry."

"No," said Lucy in a small voice. "She started it."

"Well, cheer up," said Mum. "You're going to the funfair tomorrow for your birthday treat. You'll enjoy that."

Lucy smiled a little then, but she wished Alice was coming too. It was sad not to have a best friend to go everywhere with.

The funfair was great.
Lucy went on lots of rides.

As they were leaving Lucy saw one last ride she especially wanted to go on, but it was for two children together.

Dad was too big, and Laura, her little sister, was too small.

The fair man said she could go on the ride with one of the other children in the queue. But Lucy didn't fancy that, so they went home.

"Just think," teased Dad. "You could have gone on that last ride if we'd had Alice with us."

"I don't care!" said Lucy. "I didn't want to go on that silly ride anyway."

The day before the party Lucy went with Mum to the shops. They were going to buy special treats and prizes.

"I bet Alice would like one of these," said Mum.

"And these funny wobbly things," agreed Lucy.

"It's a pity we can't get her one," sighed Mum, "but I suppose if your mind is made up, it's made up."

Lucy didn't answer. She had seen something on the other side of the window. It made her feel fluttery inside.

There was Alice, and her mum. Alice's mum was looking in a shop window, but Alice had seen Lucy. She was just about to give Lucy a big smile, but then her face went sad, and she turned away instead. Lucy felt all hot. For a moment she didn't know what to do.

Then she rushed up to Alice and gave her a huge hug.

"I'm sorry I called you bossy," said Alice, laughing.

"I'm sorry I was mean," said Lucy, "and I really, really, REALLY
want you to come to my party! Will you?"

"Yes, please!" said Alice.

And that was the end of the quarrel.

MORE LUCY AND ALICE BOOKS BY JENNIFER NORTHWAY FROM FRANCES LINCOLN

LUCY'S RABBIT

Lucy is busy making decorations for her Mum's birthday
with the help of her cousin Alice. When they discover a rabbit
eating Dad's pansies they think it is a great idea for a surprise present.
But keeping the mischievous rabbit out of trouble for long enough to give her to
Mum is much harder than they expect. And what will Mum say when she sees
what her surprise present has done to her favourite pair of slippers?

ISBN 978-1-84507-895-9

GET LOST, LAURA!

Lucy and her cousin Alice are trying to play 'Going to the Ball',
but Lucy's baby sister Laura just keeps getting in the way.
Lucy wishes she would get lost!
But when Laura really does go missing the older girls are desperate
to find her. Where can Laura be?

ISBN 978-1-84507-897-3

Frances Lincoln titles are available from all good bookshops.

You can also buy books and find out more about your favourite titles,

authors and illustrators on our website: www.franceslincoln.com